# MAGIC IS BREWING

### Book 1: Destined

## BROOKELAN ABLES

# Magic is Brewing

BOOK 1: DESTINED

by Brookelan Ables

## Published by TLM Publishing House

5905 Atlanta Highway, Alpharetta, GA.

https://www.ttpublishinghouse.com

Copyright © 2023 TLM Publishing House

To my mother, Elecca, and my teacher from high school, Mrs. Hixon.

Thank you for believing in me. I don't know where I'd be if it weren't for each of you. You were always in my corner when I needed you the most.

Do you realize, depending on the source, anywhere from 50% to 81% of people want to write a book or believe their life would be a great book?

Of that population, it would seem somewhere in the ballpark of only about 15% actually start a book. That tells me that we, as a general population, should address our self-confidence and goal-building skills because that's a lot of people who want something, know they want it, but make no effort even to start that goal.

Further, according to studyfinds.org, of those who did start their book, the number of people who actually finish a manuscript is only 8%!

In today's entertainment realm, we are experiencing the potential burnout of fresh ideas. Every story has been told, right? Some might agree with this statement, but I lean toward the opinion that while every high-level idea may have been told, there are many variations that are still held in the imagination of those who haven't yet made the decision to take a shot at their goals!

I was one of those people who assumed I wasn't good enough to write a book, so I can personally relate to those who haven't made the decision to take their shot yet.

In 2004, however, after answering the same questions repeatedly for months and hearing people saying that there should be a book out there to teach people what I was teaching them, I finally took the mentally challenging leap of faith toward writing my first book.

That book generated enough income to keep me working from home with my children for a couple of years. As a single parent, it was a true blessing.

Fast forward to modern times, technology has made self-publishing much more streamlined, but there is most definitely still a hefty learning curve involved.

The time and money lost to poor direction or errors in understanding the reader's expectations and the technical aspects of creating the book itself can take months, if not years, to truly understand.

That's where I come in. I created the I'm the Writer – Publishing Professional certification program, where I teach aspiring writers how to craft their stories and understand the research and processes required to give you a shot at your big goals! I certify writers who pass the criteria as freelance writers so they can generate an income as a ghostwriter if their passion is writing more than the marketing side.

We also help those who want to build a book around their life or a coaching program that can lend to their credibility as an expert in their field. If you would like more information, our contact information can be found at the rear of this book.

Brookelan Ables is one of the people who stepped forward and shared her dreams and goals with me. Through the interview process, I recognized a younger version of myself when I didn't have the self-confidence to take a leap of faith and bet on myself. I knew Brookelan could do this!

So many people never reach the confidence level to jump, but when you muster the courage to commit to yourself and the process, you find others are there to help lift you up. Brooke knew it wouldn't be easy, but she was committed, and she's finished her first work!

Magic is Brewing is a young-adult, short-read, supernatural romance series that encapsulates romance, fantasy, and adventure, as it provides an entertaining and magical journey for young adults.

And now, without further ado, I introduce to you Brookelan Ables, a published author!

# Contents

# Pumpkin Spice - So Nice

*Oh, Gawd, please let today not be another miserable day. I'm so sick of my life going nowhere. How can I have this super-awesome lineage of witches who came before me, and my life is so totally blah?*

*I should be happy with where my life is. I **know** this. I have a best friend who would do anything for me, but something is missing. Goddess, if you hear me, please show me my path.*

*Of course, I feel nothing after begging for a sign; I'll probably be the first witch in the family who will literally serve no purpose at all.*

Grabbing my phone, I reach out to the one person who's always had my back. I just need a little girl's time to drag me out of this funk. "Hey

Jewelz, I'm about to head out; where do you want to meet?"

"Hey, hey, Lizzy! Let's meet at The Mean Bean coffee shop by your apartment," Jewelz groaned, "But my stupid hair won't do what I want it to do!"

"Yeah, that's cool. You're lucky you're my BFF. No one else could get away with calling me that anymore. I'm a *proper* lady now that I'm an adult. I prefer Elizabeth. What are you trying to do with your hair, and why are you trying to fix it if we're just going to the coffee shop?" I ask as I walk to my closet door. I knock three times when a soft amber glow of light shines from underneath the door.

"Wait, where are you?" Jewelz asks.

"I'm in Crystal Landing trying to find some books that I need for my project." I open the door and walk into my other apartment in the human world.

"Oh, what project are you working on? Please tell me it's not the one to wake the dead! Because I'm too pretty to be in a zombie world."

"Oh, gawd no! I did that *one* time, and I will *not* be doing it again! You know how long it took to find a spell to stop them."

"Yeah, I know, and I tried to warn you!"
I lay my books and phone down and put my phone on speaker "Anyway, let me go so I can get moving. Don't take forever to do your hair I'm not in the mood to wait three hours for you."

Jewelz was silent for a moment "It doesn't take me three hours to do my hair! I'll see you there in an hour," she hung up the phone.

"Okay, so I got my books, keys, phone charger, and phone. Anything else missing?" I look around to make sure I have everything. Feeling sure I do; I walk to the coffee shop.

I love this place. As I walk in the door, the sounds and smells greet me like a warm hug. There's always a diverse assortment of people here, and I never feel like an outsider like I often do at other places here in the mortal realm.

Today, it feels especially busy. I scramble to an empty table and sit down. I lay my book down and look around to make sure no one is watching. I wave my hand over the book cover and cast a glamour spell to hide the title.

I open it and start to read when I smell something unusual. It smells like freshly cut pumpkin and apple spice, my two favorite smells. I glance up to locate the source of these divine scents that, crazy as it sounds, seem to come from this tall guy who's just walked in the front door.

When I see him, it feels like someone or something is drawing me toward him. Almost like my spirit knows him. I resist the urge to say hello. *Keep your focus on what's important*; I remind myself. A few minutes into my research, the delicious aroma wafts by me again. I look up and see the hunky guy who walked by earlier standing in from of me. His eyes are so green that they almost look forest-like.

"You don't mind if I sit, do you?" he asks with a smile.

"Oh no, you can sit I don't mind at all." *Omg, omg, keep your composure. My Gawd, why do you smell so freakin yummy?* I wonder, gazing into those green eyes of his like a deer in headlights.

"Shakespeare, huh?" he asked, looking down at my book cover. *Maybe I should have made it some trashy romance novel. It may have been more believable.*

I look at my book cover and smile, "Yes. My mother loved him. Her favorite is Romeo and Juliet. Every time she reads it, she cries."

"Brilliant taste, and I take it she's passed her love of romance onto you?" the stranger smiles, causing a tiny dimple to pop up on his gorgeous cheek. "How long have you been here in town? I've never seen you here before."

"Almost three years. You?"

"About four, I'd say. I travel a lot for my job. I used to live with my grandmother, but she decided it was time for me to get a place of my own and meet new people," he said with a laugh. "I love her to death, and suddenly, I think she's right. I'm Josh, by the way," he held his hand out for me to shake.

I smile and shake his hand, "I'm Elizabeth." The moment our hands touched, there was a zing of electricity. Part of me wanted to yank my hand back, and the other part of me wanted never to let go.

*Buzz, buzz.* The sound of my phone vibrating on the table snapped me back to the moment.

*Buzz, buzz. Buzz, buzz.*

I look at the phone, fumbling to find the button to switch it to silent mode as the notifications keep rolling in. I look back to Josh, "I'm sorry. I think my friend is trying to get a hold of me. She can be persistent at times.

Then I see her. Jewelz is sitting at a table behind Josh, giving me a big thumbs up and wearing a smile on her face that shows her approval as she points at her phone. Josh turns to see what is competing for my attention and sees my friend with her phone in the air.

"I'm guessing that's your friend?"

I smile, "Yeah, for some reason, she wants me to look at my phone."

"Go ahead and see what she wants."

I look at my phone and see five text messages from her; one saying she was on her way, another saying she was here, and two asking me who the guy is.

"She wants to know who you are." He smiles, turns around, and waves to her.

"Well, you can tell her who I am after you get to know me," he smiles. "So, you said you lived here for three years? What brought you to New York?"

Suddenly aware that anything I say beyond this point will either be a lie, or I'll scare him off if I admit I'm a witch who came to New York to figure out if I want to live like a mortal or continue the family legacy, I stare at him in silence.

"Oh, you know, growing up, finding your own direction, and all that stuff. What about you? Why did you move here?"

"Well, my father was the CEO of his own business, so after he passed away, I took over." I can see in his eyes that he hates to talk about anything to do with his father.

"I'm sorry for your loss. When I was sixteen, my grandmother passed away. After she died, I didn't know what to do with myself. It felt like I lost the only person in the world that understood what I was going through." I feel my eyes start to water, but I don't want to cry in front of my new friend. "Is it true that it's hard to be the CEO?" I blurt out to awkwardly change the subject.

He laughs a little and shakes his head, "Not really; sometimes it is, but not all the time. Like when someone doesn't do their job right and messes up something, then I have to spend hours trying to figure out what happened."

"Oh wow! That must suck." I find it incredibly comfortable talking with Josh; so much, so it surprises me.

"Oh, it does, but what can you do?" his smile lingers. *Hmm, is it getting warm in here?*

"Do you want to get out of here and go to the park down the street? Should we ask your friend?" Josh laughed but turned toward Jewelz, who was still eyes glued on the two as if she was binge-watching her favorite show on tv.

I smile, "I would like that. I'll just text her that plans changed, and she'll head home." We stand up, I pick up my book, and he reaches his hand toward me.

Normally, I would feel alarms going off throughout about how unsafe this could be, but somehow when I see his hand extended, it's perfectly natural to reach and hold it as we walk outside and toward the park.

This time, the zing of electricity spreads throughout my entire body. I don't understand what's going on, but I'm not questioning something that feels this strong and natural.

We walk to the park, and I can feel his eyes on me, "So, umm, why do you keep looking at me?"

He blushes a bit, "Sorry, it's just that I feel like I know you from somewhere, but that can't be because we've just met."

I smile and look down "When I saw you, I felt the same thing. I hope it's a good thing."

He smiles "Yeah, it's definitely a good thing. So, what other books do you like to read?"

"Are you a reader too?" I ask, getting excited, "I have so many books that I love to read that it's really hard to choose. But my favorite one has to be *Where the Heart Is*."

Josh stops walking for just a second, jaw dropped, "That's *my* favorite book, too! I couldn't put it down."

"I know, right? So big CEO of their own company, what do you do on your days off? Or do you not have days off?"

"I do, but I am still on call just in case they need me for something. My grandfather used to take me hiking and fishing when I was growing up. I really miss those days because I didn't have to worry about anything." His expression was melancholy, "What about you? What do you do for work?"

"I work around animals. Sometimes it's hard because either they want to play, or they want to run away."

"Oh wow! Are you a vet or something?"

"No, I work in an animal shelter. It's fun to work there, but there's this one cat, Noah. Clearly, he doesn't like me very well."

He laughs "What do you mean he doesn't seem to like you?"

"Well, it's like, I walk in, and there he is sitting in the chair that I sit on every day. When I go to pet him, he jumps down. When I try to talk to people, he will hiss at me like I've done something wrong." I throw my arms up, "Oh, and that's not the best part. He tries to eat my lunch!"

Josh can't stop laughing "I'm sorry it's not funny, but it is. It sounds like he picked his person. Does he do that with anyone else?"

"Not that I'm aware of. Seems like it's just me, which sucks."

"How long has he been in the shelter?"

"They said he showed up the same day I started, so maybe close to three years?"

"Well, I hear cats pick their people. If I were a cat, I know I'd pick you too!" He leans in toward me, then steps back a bit and put his hands in his pockets.

"Well, if that's true, why would he steal my food?" I look at him with a raised eyebrow.

"Maybe he thinks that your food is his food too? Maybe he wants to share it with you? Does he bring you dead animals like birds or mice?"

"Yeah, actually, he does, which is gross."

"When a cat does that, I believe it means they love you and consider you part of their family. Anyway, what do you do on your off days?"

"I usually do something with Jewelz. Sometimes we go out and have a girl's day or just stay home and watch Netflix."

"Oh, so that's what girls do when the guys are gone." he smiles.

I laugh and shake my head, "Not all the time. We sometimes talk about our lives and what we want to do with our futures and stuff."

"Ahhh, and what do *you* want to do with your life?"

I stop because, other than Jewelz, no one has ever asked me that before, "I dunno, I always wanted to own my own flower shop. I love flowers. My favorite ones are roses, but they are out of season."

I look at him, and I can tell he is pondering what season roses grow in, "Which is?"

"Late Spring and early Fall," I answer matter-of-factly. I look at him and raise my eyebrow, "Why?"

Josh beams, "So I know what to get you when we go on our first date."

A smile spreads across my face "How do you know I will say yes?"

"I don't, but I hope you will when I ask you out. If not, that's okay; I'm a patient man," his dimple peeps out at me again, causing me to elevate my playful banter.

"You know you're a really confident person."

"I know! My grandmother always tells me that If I want a girlfriend, I need to stop being so overconfident. I was worse growing up, but now I only let it show around people I like."

"Oh?" Elizabeth added, "You should have seen me growing up. I was a total hellion. I always gave my parents heart attacks. I would ride my bike down this steep hill and crash into the back of my mother's car! I'd go back in the house with cuts and scratches on my arms and legs and holes in my jeans. My mom would be livid, but somehow, she'd always end up laughing when I'd tell her what I'd done."

"Oh wow, so you really were a rebel. I remember one time I took my grandmother's car for a joy ride, and when I got home, she was sitting outside waiting for me. If looks could kill, I would have been dead long ago because that look scared the crap out of me," Josh chuckles as he shares his memory.

I start to laugh "I would have loved to see that. You don't look like the type of guy to take their grandmother's car on a joy ride, but maybe you are." We enjoy a comfortable silence as we walked the sidewalk route.

Then it happens. He touches my little finger with his hand. I can't tell if it was intentional or if he'd just brushed into my hand, but I'm just certain that I felt a soft grasp. Without a second thought, I entwine my fingers into his hand and ask, "So you like hiking, and you took your grandmother's car for a joy ride. What else do you do?"

He blew out some air "Well, I love to go to parks because it's so peaceful. I mostly go after dark because no one is there, and it's the only time I can calm my brain down after a hard day at work. What are the things you love the most about New York?" Josh smiles as he firms the grip of my hand in his. Yup, I'm holding hands with a total stranger, but somehow it feels like we've known each other forever.

"I haven't seen much of New York. The only things I've done since I moved here are work or hang out with Jewelz. And, of course, now I've been to this park with you."

"Are you telling me that you've lived here for three years and haven't done anything exciting? You haven't even been to the Statue of Liberty?"

"Shocker, right? I know, but nope. There are a lot of things on my to-do list, though. I always wanted to go to the Natural History Museum and take a carriage ride and have dinner on the dinner cruise ship. That would be the best night ever." I can feel my cheeks hurting from how much I have been smiling. Suddenly, I wonder if I've said too much or sounded too needy or desperate.

"I-"

>> Buzz Buzz<<

We both hear his phone. With pursed lips, he takes his phone out "I'm so sorry, but I have to get back to work. Something has come up."

"It's ok. I still need to hang out with Jewelz anyway," I flash a forced, no-worries smile and wonder if he sees my disappointment. I already hate his job.

"But I still owe you that date. Maybe tomorrow night I can take you out and show you New York?" Josh asks. No sooner are the words out of his mouth, I have to contain myself to avoid jumping into his arms.

"I would love that. Here is my number so you can call or text me whenever." I smile and write down my number on a napkin I pull from my purse. I don't even care if it's clean at that moment.

"I'm looking forward to it."

# Magic is Brewing

# A Magical Beginning

We go in different directions. It is shockingly painful to watch him walk away. He isn't smiling anymore. Whatever his job is, clearly, I prefer him when he's not thinking about work. I grab my phone and call Jewelz.

"Tell me every detail! What happened? Did he ask you out?" before I can even say hello, I'm getting the twenty-questions game.

I giggle, "Hello to you too, and yes, he did. We are going out tomorrow night, I think. We totally lost track of time. He got a call from work or something, or we'd probably still be walking, hand-in-hand into the…oh wow, literally, into the sunset. I had no idea it got so late!

"You want me to come and get you?" Jewelz offers.

"Nah, I'm good. I can make a portal or something, but I'll definitely need you to come over tomorrow to help me get ready for my date. I have no idea what to wear!" I walk down a dark alley to make sure no one sees me open a portal to get to my apartment.

"Yeah, what time tomorrow do you want me to head over?"

"I don't want you over super early. How about one or two in the afternoon so I can sleep in? I definitely don't wanna get sleepy on my big night out!"

"Yeah, I can do that. See you tomorrow."

##

I wake up to my phone ringing. Unknown caller. I wonder if it's him.

"Hello?"

"Hey, it's Josh I was wondering if I can pick you up at four for our date?"

"Umm, yes, that'll be great." I smile.

"Ok perfect I'll be there at four."

"Did you want to meet at the coffee shop, or were you actually going to pick me up?" I calmly ask him. He seemed anxious to get off the phone, but honestly, I feel this charge between us, like both our energies, are firing in all directions. "I'll text you my address. Will that work?"

"Yes, that'll be great. Sorry, I'm just excited, I guess," he hangs up the phone, and I immediately call Jewelz.

"Red Alert! He's going to be here to pick me up at four, so I need you to wake up. It's already two!"

I can hear Jewelz groan "Fine, but there better be coffee when I get there."

"There will be." I hang up the phone and head to the kitchen to make coffee. Five minutes later, I can hear Jewelz walking through my coat closet.

"OMG, why do you have so many jackets? I'm pretty sure you don't even wear most of them."

"Hey, I wear them! Just not the ones with tags on them still. I usually get them because I think I have an outfit for them. The coffee is almost ready, so pour yourself a cup and come upstairs I'm going to take a shower."

"Okay, I'll start laying the clothes out that I know will look good on you for your first date with Josh." Jewels' words come out in a teasingly sweet sing-songy voice, but I can tell she's as excited for me as I am!

As promised, when I come out of the shower, there's a lineup of outfits that Jewelz has picked out. "Okay, so it's three thirty! We need to fix my hair and do a little bit of makeup. I sure hope he likes a natural look because there's no time for glam today!"

"I think you need to curl your hair and just a little bit of lipstick," Jewelz plugs in the curling iron. "So, I was doing a little bit of research on Josh. You know, just to make sure he's not an ax murderer. But I came across something super weird," Jewelz looked at me like she'd just read a shocking headline on a trashy tabloid.

"Okay, out with it! What'd you see?" I could feel my pulse beating in my chest now. What the heck!

"Do you remember a family called the Benedetto?" she quizzed.

Now thoroughly confused, "A little." I reply, "My mother used to talk about them and how sad it was that they passed away at such young ages."

"Wait, how old were they?" Jewelz asked as she checked the temp on the hot iron.

"What I understood from my mom is that the parents were like 36 and 37, and the son was sixteen when they died. No one knows what happened to him though. They think he left because he didn't know how to deal with the loss of his parents. Why do you ask?"

"Well, the research I found said that like a hundred years ago the **Audra** family, that's *your* family, and a family called the Benedetto coven worked together to bring down an evil warlock of the Norwood coven. I guess he was trying to destroy our town.

So, when they vanquished him, it's believed that the entire Norwood coven disappeared the same day. But there's an urban legend that they swore that they would be back after one hundred years, and they would be stronger than ever." Jewelz was in her glory when she was retelling the old family stories. It was definitely interesting, but I need her to focus on not burning my hair.

"But why would my family hide the fact that they fought the Norwood coven?" I wonder aloud, trying not to get upset with them.

"Maybe they were trying to protect you from it. Because of how bad they are. Who knows, but wow, right?" Jewelz sits down on the end of the bed "Besides, they probably don't worry about it because they don't believe the Norwood would actually come back. It could be fake to scare people."

We hear the doorbell ring, and I start to feel the butterflies in my belly change from fluttering to stomping on my stomach.

"Jewelz please go get the door, and if it's Josh, tell him that I'm almost ready. I just need to calm myself down for a few minutes."

Jewelz gets up and goes downstairs. I finish the final curl in my hair from where Jewelz left off. Thankfully, she did the back, and I look like a freakin rockstar. I check myself in the mirror and wonder why I don't get dressed up more often, but hey, maybe if I actually string some dates together, I may!

I walk downstairs to see Josh and Jewelz talking. Josh looks at me, his face beaming, "You look so beautiful."

I feel flushed, "Thank you. You look amazing too!"

He walks to me and hands me the most gorgeous roses. They're such a deep red color inside, and the vibrancy brightens at the tip. "They're beautiful! I thought they were out of season! How did you get them?" I take a whiff, and they smell like they just bloomed.

"They are, but my grandmother has a greenhouse. She has a magic touch with flowers. When I told her I'd met the most beautiful woman in the city and that she loves roses, Gram had them couriered over to me immediately. They're literally just clipped."

I smile up at him "They are wonderful. Thank you so much. Please thank your grandmother for me too! I'm going to put these in a vase and then we can go."

I walk to the kitchen and grab a vase, add a bit of sugar water, and the flowers. *If the rest of the day is going to be this magical, this may be the best night of my life!*

I walk back to where Josh and Jewelz awkwardly await my return, "Okay, I'm ready, let's go." I walk to the door and grab my purse and jacket. Josh and I walk outside to his car. He opens the passenger door for me. *Well, well, well, I didn't think anyone still opens doors for ladies.*

I look at him and smile, "Thank you. So, where are we going?" I look at him and see an almost sly grin on his face. This is all so exciting!

"You'll see when we get there. I really hope you like it," he teases.

"If you're going to be there, I'm pretty sure I'll like it," I've never considered myself a flirt, but everything out of my mouth just seems to fly out before I can stop it with this guy. There's definitely something different about him.

We get to where we are going, and he pulls into a parking spot "Okay, I need you to close your eyes," I smile, but he's looking at me without flinching.

"Wait, are you serious?" a bit uncomfortable without even knowing where we are, and now he wants me to close my eyes. "Why do you want me to close my eyes?"

"Come on, please, it's a surprise," he whines. I must be completely smitten with this guy because never in my life has a man's whining made me feel excited to my core as it does right now.

"Okay, they're closed." I can hear him open and shut his door, scurry around, and within seconds, I feel my door open.

"I'm going to hold your arm and help you out if that's okay with you?" Even when he tells me what he's going to do, he does it in such a kind way. I realize I'm not going to be able to tell this man no to anything.

I smile blindly, "Yes. Thank you." I put my hand out so he can gently help me upright. I feel his hand on mine, and again, there is that electricity that I've never felt before with anyone. Clearly, it isn't because of where we were before if it's still happening. It's something in him… or is it us?

"Okay, I need you to step out of the car but be careful."

I step out of the car, and suddenly I can smell the ocean, "Are we by the ocean? Have I dressed appropriately?"

I move around a little but still keep a hold of him. I hear him shut the door and lock it, "Yes, we are. You can open your eyes."

With excitement I haven't felt since I was a kid at Christmas, I open my eyes and scan left to right. I see a ferry, a beautiful view, and a few couples walking along the beach. What are we going to do? This is better than my wildest dream, and it's barely even started yet!

Josh smiles, then giggles. Within seconds, he's outright laughing… at me! "What are you laughing at?" I demand, hands on waist.

"I'm sorry, it's just the way your face looked for a second. It looked like you were confused and surprised, but it is just so adorable."

I feel my blood start to boil up from being embarrassed. "Are we here to take me out on a date or to make fun of me?" I snipped playfully. *Clearly, I'm not able to be mad at him, either. It's almost like he has me charmed. But I'm the witch here, not him.*

He smiles back at me and takes my arm "This way, my lady, we are going to see the Statue of Liberty, the second most beautiful woman in the United States."

We get on the ferry. My gawd, the water is so beautiful. I soak in the smells and sounds and just how fiercely valiant she stands. My eyes begin to feel misty. *Oh, come on, not now. Don't wreck your makeup with tears on the first date!*

I feel Josh put his arm on my waist. It's clear that he's not making a move on me when I smile and see his eyes beginning to well up at the literal majesty of where we are standing.

If I had to describe my feeling at this moment, the closest emotion would just be *full*. If this is a dream, I never want to wake up.

"She's gorgeous," I say to break the silence.

"Yes, she is. Did you know the statue sways three inches in the wind, and the torch sways five inches?"

"How do you know that?" I ask, suddenly remembering the Hitch movie when the main character had researched the history to impress a first date. *He doesn't seem like the type to research just to impress someone, but even if he did, it works. I'm impressed!*

"I like to read history books, but mostly because I did a report on the Statue of Liberty back in junior high. I got an A+ on it, and this has been one of my favorite spots since," Josh smiles and held out his hand.

We walk to the top of the crown, "Okay, smarty-pants, tell me what the seven points on the crown represent."

He smiles, "They represent the seven continents of the world. Did you know that they say that under her crown, there is a secret box concealed, and inside the box is a copy of the U.S. Constitution, a portrait of the statue's designer, and twenty bronze medals?"

"I did not. You definitely deserved that A+ back then and an A+ for the best date ever tonight!" I swear, I never wear my heart on my sleeve like I am with Josh, but something just feels so right…natural.

I can't help but feel butterflies when I'm near him. Next, we went to the Museum of Natural History and took a carriage ride that dropped us off at the pier for a dinner cruise. *This is unbelievable. Could this evening get any better?*

\#\#

"So, how long did you plan this date?" I asked while trilling my fork in my spaghetti.

"Honestly? Only a couple hours," he smiles at me, "I remember you saying you always wanted to visit the Statue of Liberty, go to the Museum, have a carriage ride, and a dinner cruise. See? I listen well!"

He is making me feel like a schoolgirl again. After dinner, he drives me to my house and walks me to my front door.

"I had a lot of fun tonight," He smiles while putting a piece of my hair behind my ear.

I try not to appear too eager but can't help but beam brightly. His fingers felt so soft on my cheek "I did too." I reach for his hand and, for the first time, felt something cold on his finger, "What is this?"

He looks down to where our hands meet and realizes I am asking about his ring. "It's a family ring. We get them when we turn sixteen."

*Oh my gosh, no, no, no. Is it possible? How did I miss it?* "Are you in a coven?" I ask, knowing that his response may change everything for us both.

His eyes dart straight to mine, I can see he's wondering how I would know this from a ring. We both stand in silence for what feels like an eternity as we both plot our next actions based on each other's responses. Oh, my Gawd, what did Jewelz say about all that family history stuff? Why didn't I listen to her?

"Yes. But how did you know?"

I show him my ring that I keep around my neck "Because I'm also a witch. I come from a long bloodline of Audra and Atwater."

*Please do not let our covens be at war. I couldn't survive not seeing this beautiful face again. There's no turning back now. I've already thrown out our lineage, so now I wait to see who your family is.*

I can see in his eyes that he is surprised and perhaps a bit relieved himself, "My grandmother always talked about you guys like your family were the queen and king of Crystal Landing! Your family helped my grandmother when she needed it the most." Relief spread through my spirit. *Thank you, Goddess.* "What's your family's name?"

"My mother's name was Aiken, and my father's name was Benedetto."

This time it was my turn to look taken back "OMG! Before you walked up to me at the coffee shop, I was doing research, and your family and mine fought together to bring down the Norwood family."

"Yeah, my grandmother told me stories about how your family helped my family." His gaze connects with mine, and we both stand entranced, locked into each other's spirits. *Has fate brought us together? Or is this just a coincidence?*

"I think I'm going to kiss you now." He starts to lean in.

"I think I'm going to kiss you now, too." I lean in, and when our lips connect, I feel my powers explode inside of me. We pull apart when my porch light shatters, and I scream like a little girl.

We look at each other and laugh, "That's definitely the first time anything like this has happened to me." I'm not sure if I'm embarrassed or excited at the energy that pulses between us. Clearly, we have a connection.

"Same here," Josh agrees, "But I think that's a good thing. I'm going to head to my grandmother's house to visit. She will never believe who my girlfriend is."

"So, I'm your girlfriend now? I like it." I walked into my house and shut the door. I leaned my back against the door, "I love today."

# Six Month Anniversary

We have been dating for almost six months. Tonight, I ask Josh to come with me to my work party at a bar down the street from the shelter. Of course, he said yes, which is yet another reason why I'm seriously falling for this guy. He's always down for going out with my friends, even if it does end up being an evening of crazy cat stories.

"Wait, let me get this straight! Noah, the cat, bites you? What do you do?" I asked Jewelz while trying to hold back a laugh.

She looks at me with her best *duh* face, "I didn't do anything! I picked him up to love on him and the next thing I know he bites me and off he runs." At this point, I can't hold my laugh in anymore and let out a true cackle.

When josh came back to our table with some drinks, "What're you ladies laughing about?" he smiles, "I need to hear all the juicy details!"

"Jewelz is just telling me what happened at work with Noah." I can't help but laugh again. Through the laughter, we both hear a familiar sound. Our mouths drop open, and we both squeal like little girls!

"OMG, I haven't heard this song in forever!" Jewelz says, grabbing my hand to take me to the middle of the dance floor just in time for the *everybody clap your hands* part. Of course, Jewelz is a pro. She's perfect at everything. But somewhere along the line, I missed out on the rhythm gene, so I laugh along with everyone else as they all show me how to clap to the beat. What can I say? It just didn't come naturally, and so far, I haven't found a spell to teach me how to clap.

When the song ends, I look over at Josh and see him talking to a strange girl. It's very clear that he knows her. I walk over and hear Josh, "Why are you here?"

The girl rubs her hand down Josh's arm, "I heard you would be here and want to say how sorry I am for how we broke up and want to try again if you want to."

She is getting too close for comfort for me. Whoever she is, I decide to put a stop to this right now! I grab her hand and drop it off of his arm and replace my hand on his arm "Hey Babe, everything okay over here?" I ask in the sweetest voice I can muster, making eye contact with this person, wondering why Josh never mentioned her before, but making it clear, that she's his past, not his present.

She returns my glare. In fact, she may be able to out-cat me in that department. I feel a pang of intimidation as I look her up and down with disgust. She's absolute perfection. No wonder he didn't mention her to me. He knows me well enough to know I'd be insecure about knowing he was with someone so gorgeous.

"Joshi-Pooh," she said in a slow and pouty voice, "who is this girl? I thought you said ours is a forever love?"

Josh looks at this unwelcome stranger, and I can feel the energy change, "Elizabeth, this is an old friend, Kathy. Kathy, this is my girlfriend, Elizabeth." He looks at me and smiles.

Kathy starts to laugh, "A new girlfriend?" she looks at me, clearly judging, "You can't have been around very long. Joshi and I talk all the time, and he's never as much as *mentioned* you, and now, you're his *girlfriend*? Have you even met his grandmother yet? She loves me to death. Trust me, she'll hate you. She only wants the best for her grandson, and we agree that's me!" Kathy rolls her upper lip in disgust toward me.

I hate the way she makes me feel. My eyes start to burn. I can't cry. Stay strong. I realize it's a losing battle as I feel a tear escape. I can't let anyone see me cry, so I turn away from them both. Jewelz notices the commotion, "What's going on here? Does someone need to be turned into a toad?" She asks jokingly.

"As if you could," Kathy bites back at Jewelz, making it clear that Kathy is not a welcome visitor. Jewels glances toward me. I can tell her empathetic senses are on full alert. While I usually love that she can sense my emotions, at this moment, seeing her expression of sorrow toward me, I am overcome with such a feeling of loss and hopelessness, it's all I can do to try to stand my ground.

Josh looks at Kathy, "You need to leave before I make you leave."

"Come on Joshi, let's get out of here. We can go back to my place," Kathy attempts to tease Josh by swirling her fingers in his hair.

I can't even wait for his answer. I feel sick to my stomach. I need air. I look back to Jewelz in despair, and I run. Of course, we're at the back side of the bar, and I don't have the sense to run out the front door, so I run to the nearest familiar door I see. The ladies' bathroom.

Jewelz runs into the bathroom right behind me, "Awe, bestie it's okay!" she hugs me gently. I'm shaking and sweating and bawling like a small child torn away from her favorite pony.

"No, it's not. We were having the best night until that bitch showed up and ruined everything," Jewelz can't help but laugh "Why are you laughing?"

"Because we're both in a shitty situation," I look around at where we are and can't help but laugh through the tears, "We *are* in a bathroom and the only thing you can think of is to crack jokes? Girl, I'd be lost without you! Thanks."

She looks at me and wipes my tears away, "It made you laugh, didn't it?"

I nod, "Yeah, it did. I think I want to go home and forget today ever happened."

Jewelz helps me up, "I think that's a great idea. Maybe we can stop at The Sassy Cow and grab some ice cream on the way? "

We walk to the door and try to open it but it's locked. I look at her, "Did you lock the door when you came in?"

"No, how can I? There's no lock on the door," Jewelz says while still trying to open the door.

I don't know how, but I know who's to blame. "I think I know who did this."

Jewelz steps back from the door and looks at me. "Who? That girl? How could she though?"

I can see Jewelz face turning red, "That stupid skank. She's so lucky I'm not out there I would turn her into a frog for real!"

I remember a spell that can open locked doors. I wave my hand over to the handle, and it unlocks, "How in the world did you do that?" Jewelz asks.

"Didn't you ever pay attention in school?" I look at Jewelz, "While you were out flirting with the boys, I was doing my homework."

"Zero regrets on choosing boys over history and lame spells that you'll never use... Well, unless some dumb hoe locks you in a public bathroom, anyway."

I roll my eye's at her and walk out of the bathroom. Out of the corner of my eye, I see Josh standing at the bar. I'm in no condition to face him right now. We walk by him in silence, Jewelz leading me by the hand, toward the door. I hear him calling my name. Jewelz tightens her grip on my hand as she senses my hesitation, "Just ignore him and keep walking. You can talk to him tomorrow after you've had time to calm down a bit." I listen obediently, and we walk to my car.

# Magic is Brewing

# Ready to Make Nice

It's been a week since the bar, and I feel bad for not talking to Josh, but I don't know how to tell him about my insecurities. *'Sorry, Josh, but I haven't had a ton of boyfriends and never had to fight for one.' Yeah, that'll go over well.*

Buzz, Buzz… I look to see Josh's name on the caller ID. For the first time in a week, I decide to answer.

"Hello?"

I can hear Josh sighing, "Elizabeth I've been calling you for a week! I was worried because you haven't been answering your phone or texts."

I can't help but tear up a little. He really misses me. I try to keep my voice calm, "I-I'm sorry I just didn't feel like talking about what happened at the bar. I didn't like the way she was talking down to me."

It was silent for a moment, "I'm sorry babe, I really didn't know she would show up but if it makes you feel better I was fixing to turn her into a frog," he laughs nervously, and I can't help but smile as well, "Jewelz said the same thing."

"Well, I guess great brains think alike."

We cautiously start to talk about safe topics like work and the weather, but then an awkward silence takes over, "I have to tell you something because I'm pretty sure my past is coming back to haunt me, and I need to tell you before it does."

"It's okay you can tell me anything you want. I won't judge you," as the words escape my mouth, I have to wonder if I'm assuring Josh or myself.

"After my parents passed away, I fell into a dark place. I started to act differently. I was making a lot of crappy choices and sleeping around when I met Kathy. I thought I loved her. The more I got to know her, I started to realize that she was doing dark magic."

"Oh, my Gawd, so she's a witch too? No wonder she responded to Jewelz about the toad comment without a reaction! I should have recognized that" I interrupted, "I'm sorry, please continue."

"Yeah, most of my life has been back in Briarwood Flats, and that's where I met Kathy. I thought she was different. Well, she's different all right! Anyway, it got to the point where she was hurting people, and I didn't want to have anything to do with any of that type of magic, or her either. I broke up and decided to move to New York, and then I meet you. With you, it's nothing like the feelings I had with her. With you, it's totally different. Every time I'm with you I feel my heart race and my hands sweat. I even get this zap of energy pulse through my entire body when we touch. If I'm not near you or talking to you, I feel like I'm a lost soul without a purpose."

I can't help but cry. This time, they're happy tears. I feel my powers go crazy and I'm so aware of the emotions that I don't realize Josh is still trying to talk to me, "Elizabeth, you, okay? I can feel something is wrong."

"Yeah, I'm sorry I just feel so happy. I appreciate you telling me this. I have to ask you something," I ask, afraid of his response, but knowing I have to find out, "Do you really think your grandmother will hate me? I'd like to meet her. You speak so highly of her, but so did Kathy. I'm afraid now that she may not like me."

"Are you crazy? She hates Kathy. Ignore literally everything that Kathy told you. She was trying to break us apart. Nothing was true. My grandmother will adore you! What about tomorrow? I know for a fact she's dying to meet you."

"I'd like that."

We stay on the phone for several hours, even to the point that we both are in our beds, talking about our plans for the next few weeks. Realizing my phone is about to die, I thank Josh for being patient with me about being so sensitive.

"Are you kidding, I should be thanking you for being so forgiving of my drama. You really mean a lot to me. I don't want to lose what we have," and the battery went dead.

What a perfect place to end the conversation, I think to myself as I drift off to sleep with a smile on my face.

##

>>Ding Ding

*Oh man, is that him already?* I glance into the mirror and rush to the front door. *Deep breath. Don't appear overly anxious.* I swing open the door, and there he is, wearing shorts and a polo shirt.

Before I can say anything, he grins at me like a boy on a first date, pushes a bouquet of what must be two or three dozen of the reddest roses toward me, and says, "I'm so glad to see you. It's been hellish without you the past week. I swear you look more beautiful every time I see you."

I can't help but feel flushed, "Thank you, you look handsome. Please come in I just need to put my shoes and jacket on and then I'll be ready to go." I let him in and walk to my closet and grab my shoes and jacket.

"Okay, I'm ready." I walk to the living room, where I see josh and Noah playing, "I see you adopted him?" Josh smiles at me, and before I can respond, I hear a voice that I know for a fact didn't come from Josh or me.

"She didn't have a choice."

Josh and I look around, and then we look at each other.

"I'm down here."

I look down and see Noah looking up at me.

"Is he grinning?" I ask Josh.

"Did you just talk?" I awkwardly look at Noah and ask.

"Yes, I did, and thank God, you finally understand me. Do you know how much the cat food you buy me sucks?"

"Hey, that's the best-rated cat food in the world, and it's good for you!" I look at Noah, scoldingly, and then look to Josh, "I can't believe I'm arguing with my cat!"

"Good for me? You people need to fire whoever is rating it. It sucks! Anyway, be careful today. I have a bad feeling something is going to happen," Noah warned and then nonchalantly walked away.

Josh and I stare, dumbfounded, "So I guess I have a talking cat."

"Yeah, you do but I think it's more than a cat. I think you found your familiar." Josh said, walking to the front door.

"Well, that's exciting and weird. I'm going to have to do some research about this! I hope he's wrong that something bad will happen today. I don't think we can handle any more drama this soon!"

Josh mumbled something under his breath that I couldn't hear, but I didn't question it. We drove to a wooded area, and Josh says a spell that opens a portal.

*In Briarwood Flats, a magic land,*
*A portal waits for your hand,*
*With a wave and a spell, you'll be on your way,*
*To a place where dreams come al–*

As I hear Josh speak the magical words, I can't help but interrupt, "Wait, you're from Briarwood Flats? I'm from Crystal Landing! No wonder our families fought together in the past. How in the world have we lived our entire lives in neighboring villages and never met?"

Josh smiles, unsure what the answer is himself, "I have no idea. Maybe it wasn't our time to meet yet. I'm just glad that we're together now. Now, let me try that spell again."

*"In Briarwood Flats, a magic land,*
*A portal waits for your hand,*
*With a wave and a spell, you'll be on your way,*
*To a place where dreams come alive and play."*

Unlike my portals, which usually radiate a slight amber tone, I notice that Josh's portal is more of a green tone. I wonder if that means anything, but it seems normal to him, so I just take his hand and he drives us into the portal.

"I have to be honest; I'm kind of nervous."

"Don't be. My grandmother has been wanting to meet you, and when I told her I'm bringing you today, she was over the moon."

There is a rush of exhilaration followed by an immediate calmness. I don't have a clue how I can feel such different emotions at the same moment, but I love how it feels just to be near him.

We pull up to a house with a metal black gate with a B in the middle. "Here we are! Are you ready?"

I see sparks come out of my fingertips, "Yeah, just really nervous."

We get out of the car and walk to the front door. Josh pushes the door open, and before we can get in fully into the entry hall, someone pulls me in for a hug, "Oh sweet pea, she looks so pretty, and look at those eyes! They're the same as her mother's."

Taken aback, "You knew my mother?"

"Of course, dear, your family and mine knew each other for years. You think you found each other by accident?"

"Well, yes, I thought it was a coincidence that we found each other, but now you have me wondering!" I admit as I examine this woman's kind face. Her eyes held so much wisdom; I feel intoxicated by her presence.

His grandmother smiles and walks deeper into the house, "Please, come in and sit anywhere you like."

When I stepped into the house, I didn't feel nervous anymore. I smile at Josh. "I think I'm going to like it here."

Josh takes my jacket and hangs it up before we go into the living room to sit down. A moment later, his grandmother walks in with tea. "I hope you like tea because that's mostly all I drink around here." She laughs, and I can't help but giggle softly.

"You have the most beautiful smile ever, dear. I can tell you make Josh incredibly happy, unlike that bitch Sandy or whatever her name is. I never liked her from the start. Her energy gave me the creeps. But you, I can feel that you are different, but in a good way."

I can't help but smile, "Thank you, Mrs. Benedetto."

She looks at me, shocked. Her gaze turns from me and then toward Josh. With a look that could kill, she accuses, "You didn't tell her that she could call me Gram-Gram?"

I muffle a giggle and look down. I'm not sure if she's teasing him or seriously upset, I hope the former.

"No, he didn't." I laugh at her reaction.

"Well, from this moment on, you call me Gram-Gram, nothing more, nothing less."

"Yes, Gram-Gram." I look at Josh. His expression assures me that Gram-Gram will always be an unpredictable barrel of laughs.

Ding.

"Oh, my cookies, I'll be right back dears," she gets up and walks to the kitchen, and I look back at Josh with a smile "I think she likes me."

Josh smiles back, "Yeah, she does. You're the first girlfriend I've brought over that she's said that to, not to mention, the most beautiful one."

*I love this man.*

##

*Ding-Dong*

"Can someone get that for me, please!" Gram-Gram yells from the kitchen.

"Yes, ma'am," Josh calls out as he gets up and walks to the front door. When he opens it, I can feel the energy change in the room, and I hear yelling. I get up and see Kathy at the door.

She looks at me, then at Josh, and kisses him on the mouth like they are still a couple. Josh pulls away and starts to plead his case to me, but I know what's up at this point. Josh isn't doing this. It's all her little game.

Kathy rolls her eyes at Josh and walks toward the living room like she's in familiar territory. She doesn't even look at me as she passes. "Josh, I see you're still trying to make me jealous of this woman you're dating. But don't worry. I'll take you back."

Before I could say something, Gram-Gram walks in while drying her hands, "Who's at the door, sweetheart?" she looked at Kathy, and I could feel her shift, "What in the hell are you doing here?" Gram-Gram demanded with a look that could burn.

Kathy looks shocked but smiles and put her hand on her heart. "Gram-Gram, I just came to see you and visit with my boyfriend, Josh."

Gram-Gram didn't like the fact that she was in her house uninvited, "That's Mrs. Benedetto to you," she walked straight toward Kathy, leaving them nose to nose, "You have three seconds to leave my house and never come back before I force you to leave!"

Kathy started to laugh, "Josh wanted me here, and now I see why," she said while looking me up and down. "Don't worry, dear, not everyone can look this good."

I can feel my magic flowing through my body that I haven't felt in a while. I can feel my hands start to shake, "Gram-Gram is right. You have three seconds to leave before I kick you out of her house myself!"

Kathy spins to look back toward me and laughs, "Oh, sweetheart, you're not powerful enough to throw out the trash. I promise you, you can't begin to handle –"

I didn't give her time to finish her sentence, I throw my hands up, and with a strength that I honestly didn't even realize I had in me, I woosh her out the door.

Realizing what I've done, I'm afraid to look at Gram-Gram and Josh. I can hear Gram-Gram putting a spell on her house to keep Kathy out.

"Bar the doors, lock the gates,
With this spell, I seal my fate.
Let no unwanted enter here,
Protected by the powers dear.

Spirits of the Earth and Air,
Hear my call, be my pair,
Guardians of the North and South,
Protect my home, keep it free from doubt.

By the power of three times three,
I banish all negativity,
This is my will, so mote it be,
My home is safe, so shall it be."

I listen to Gram-Gram's spell and realize why she's such a revered leader in the coven. Is it possible to already love this sweet lady already?

"Babe, are you okay?" he asks as he feverishly checks me out to make sure I'm not injured in the windstorm I whipped up.

Suddenly, the emotions of the day overcome me, and once again, I start to cry. "I've never magically fought anyone before" the emotional release caused me to feel weak in the knees.

"Hey, hey, it's okay," Josh pulls me into a hug just as I start to collapse. His strength radiates into my body, literally. I begin to feel rejuvenated as he holds me and rubs my back with smooth circles. I don't know if this is something he knows he's doing, but before I can tell him the sensation his touch is giving me, we hear someone laugh.

"That had to be the best thing I have ever seen in my whole life," Gram-Gram is standing beside us, literally dancing about the entry hall, celebrating our little victory.

Josh and I look at each other and begin laughing as well. Josh kisses my forehead and takes my hand, and spins me around as we join Gram-Gram in the celebratory dance.

"I knew you had something about you that I liked," Gram-Gram breathes a sigh of relief, "I've waited for what felt like forever for you two to find each other. I knew Josh had a destined pairing, but I couldn't tell who she was... until today."

I smile and walk over to hug her, "Thank you. I feel it too, but it just didn't seem possible."

"No need to thank me. Just have to believe in yourself, and when you do, anything is possible."

We stay a while longer, sharing stories of how each of us grew up and how many times we just barely missed each other at parades, community carnivals, or concerts.

I look at the clock and realize how late it is. "I think it's time to go. I need to feed Noah," I nod to Josh. I look at Gram-Gram, whose head is cocked a bit to the side, "Noah?"

"Yes, ma'am, he's my cat, well more like a familiar."

"That's nice that you have a familiar. They can help you through tough times and tell you if something bad is going to happen."

I stand up and hug Gram-Gram, "Thank you for having me."

I look at Josh and watch his tenderness as he kisses Gram-Gram's cheek. I wonder if he's always like this with her.

"It's no problem. You better come back and visit me! I don't care if Josh is with you or not," I smile because I believe she actually means it. Josh puts my jacket around me with a soft embrace. Yeah, I can definitely get used to this.

##

I'm out catching up on errands today while Josh is visiting his Gram-Gram. I walk outside of the Quick Stop Food Mart and immediately feel uncomfortable. I don't know what, who, or why, but someone is watching me.

I can feel a negative energy so evil that it makes me nauseous. I try to ignore it and quickly unload the cart of groceries into the trunk. I don't know what is going on, but I know I need to get home and call Josh.

As I'm driving home, a bolt of energy goes through me and my entire body is paralyzed. I don't know if it's a heart attack or a stroke or what's wrong with me, but my arms suddenly feel like they weigh a ton, and it takes every bit of strength I can muster to keep the car on the road.

~ HONK! HONK! HOOOONNNNK!

A car behind me starts to honk its horn erratically at me. *What the hell's wrong with you? Can't you see I'm having an emergency in here?* I scream out to the driver in my mind. I can't even move my mouth to scream or call anyone for help. *Maybe the car that's honking will see me if I take my foot off the gas entirely and will realize I need help!*

The car behind me seems to be pulling up beside me. I'm unsure if they're going to pass me, flip me off, or help me. The vehicle slows down to see what's going on with me. Thank Gawd! I try to move my head or blink my eyes to make some sort of sign to the passerby that I need help, and then I see her.

It's Kathy! *What the hell is she trying to do?* Suddenly, she veers her car straight into the side of my car, and I can't help but swerve while trying to keep the car on the road.

I can see her laughing. There's a curve ahead, so I try to slow down, but it's no use. My brake pedal goes straight to the floorboard of the car. *Oh, Goddess, please protect me!* I scream as I feel the car smash into the tree in front of me.

I wake up to the car horn going off, and I see Kathy get out of her car and walk toward me. She breaks my driver's side window and grabs the back of my hair,

"You better stay away from Josh I had him first, and nothing is going to stand in my way; Do you hear me?"

I feel blood dripping down my face. Every part of my body is in excruciating pain. Kathy slams my head on the steering wheel, and as my eyes close, *Oh Gawd, is this how I die?* is my final thought, as all thoughts, sounds, and feelings go black.

"Miss! Miss! Are you okay?" *Am I dead, or am I dreaming? Please let this have all been a dream.* I try to answer the voice, but I can't even muster a nod before I pass out.

# Magic is Brewing

# Am I Dead?

I wake up to a beeping noise in the background, and I smell bleach. I open my eyes and see Josh in a chair beside my hospital bed. He's sleeping with his head resting on my bed, and I can tell he's been crying.

A moment later, a nurse walked in and sees me awake "He's been here since you got here," she smiles, knowing this would be a great comfort to me.

I try to return her smile, but everything is sore. I try to move my fingers and can at least confirm that I have control over my body again– well, to some degree.

"How long have I been here?"

The nurse stops and looks at me, taking my hand in hers, "A week, dear, but thank goodness you got here when you did," she walks to the door, "I'll let a doctor know that you're awake!"

I look back to Josh and put my fingers on his head. I'm the one in the hospital bed, and all I can think of is to try to comfort him. Josh begins to wake up and tries to swat my hand away, "Hey, don't swat at me, Mr. Rude," I find the energy to tease him.

"I'm trying to sleep, Lizzy," he says, almost annoyed. Knowing what a sound sleeper he is once he gets to sleep, I tickle his ear this time. He lifts his head, and I have to assume he realizes where he's at, and with the speed of a cheetah, he goes from sound asleep to eyes bugged and both of his hands patting me on my arms and belly.

"Elizabeth? You're awake!" He hugs a bit too aggressively, causing me to let out a soft whine. "Oh God, I'm sorry, babe! I didn't mean to hurt you."

I smile, "It's okay." I feel my eyes start to burn, "Kathy did this to me, and I couldn't do anything. I felt so weak." I try not to cry, but this time, I decide I have been through enough. The release of tears feels therapeutic. Josh doesn't shush me like a tiny baby this time, either. He nods, holds my hand, and runs his hand along my hair, wiping away my tears as needed. "You are *not* weak, babe, okay? Don't ever think that. None of us knew this was going to happen, and if I had, I would have done something to help you. I'm so sorry that I brought her into our lives." He kisses my forehead and smiles. I feel the depth of his pain and know he blames himself.

A moment later, a doctor comes in with a clipboard, "So, I hear our patient is awake," he smiles at me as he reads my chart and checks the vitals and machine readings, "You have some nasty bumps and bruises, but thankfully, there doesn't appear to be anything broken. I want to keep you overnight to make sure you are okay, but if all goes well, we'll send you two home tomorrow."

"Yes, sir. Thank you. Could you find any reason why I couldn't move right before the accident? I mean, did I have a stroke or anything?" Realizing it was probably a spell from Kathy, I quickly backpedaled, "Honestly, I'm not even sure what was real or imagined at this point. Thank you, doctor."

The doctor looked at me, a bit puzzled, but discounted my question almost as quickly as I took it back. If Kathy put a paralysis spell on me, that's something we'll take care of on our own. I reminded myself.

I didn't realize Josh was still holding my hand until he let it go. I look at Josh and smile, "I'm sorry I scared you."

He kisses my forehead, "It's okay. It absolutely isn't your fault," his jaw clenches, and I feel a rage building inside him.

"How did you know I was here?"

He smiles, "Jewelz called me and said that you were in the hospital, so I rushed straight here."

He can tell that I'm getting sleepy again. He pulls the blanket up to my shoulders, bends over, and kisses my forehead again, "I'll be here when you wake up."

"Good, my forehead is getting a lot more kisses than my lips are. When I wake up, I expect you to do something about that. But we'll have to revisit this conversation when my eyes agree to stay open,"

Whatever pain medication they're giving me, I feel like my mind is fully alert, but my body is exhausted. I try to look into his eyes, but my eyes are too heavy. "I love you," I whisper.

##

"I know I should have asked first, but I put a protection spell over your house so Kathy can't harm you anymore," Josh looks at me sheepishly on the drive home from the hospital, "I just refuse to sit back and let her get away with this. She's going to pay for this, and it will be on our terms, not mortal laws!"

"Thanks, Babe," I kiss his hand that I've been holding, "We definitely agree on that point, she won't just go away, and we can't let her keep hurting people like this." Josh leans over to try to sneak a real kiss at a stop light. I see him coming, so I turn to meet him in the middle.

~ BONK

"Ow!" I comically shriek as I raise my hand to the big goose egg on my forehead from where Kathy slammed my head into the steering wheel.

"Damn, babe, I'm so sorry. I'm so clumsy. I shouldn't have tried that with you in the shape you're in," Josh chastises himself as he starts to pull away from me.

"Wait, wait, stop! You're not getting away from me that easily. Turn back over here, and let's figure out how to do this right. I'm not about to stop kissing you until my whole body heals!"

We awkwardly align our bodies and faces while still at the stoplight to make sure we get at least one good kiss in before the light turns green again. There it is, that buzz of electricity again. The energy transfer I get from his touch is like nothing I've experienced with anyone before. No matter how many times we kiss, it still feels like the first time we kissed on my front porch.

"There you go! See, I knew we could figure it out," I tease Josh as I create a heart with my hands to let him know we can still be fun and playful. I sense his feelings of guilt so strongly that I determine that I'm going to assure him I don't hold him responsible for this at all.

"So, this is going to seem weird, but every time we kiss, like from day one, I feel this electrical energy surge into my body. I felt silly bringing it up before. I dunno, I thought it was my inexperience or something, but believe it or not, I really feel like you transfer energy into my body when you kiss me. I truly feel stronger just from that kiss. I propose we experiment with my theory a bit more when we get back to my place. Deal?"

"Deal!" Josh quickly responds as he gazes into my eyes, "You're so damn beautiful. It tears me up inside to see all these bumps and bruises, knowing you got hurt because of me. I'll never forgive myself for this," Josh notices the light has turned green again, and we drive forward in silence for a bit.

"Listen, I don't want to have to say this again. We both know why I got hurt, and it is absolutely not your fault. I just told you that your kisses are healing, so how about we focus on you being responsible for healing me for the rest of the day instead of worrying about something that's already behind us? So just say something positive or nice, and let's move forward!"

By the time I finish my sentence, I can tell that neither of us is sure if I'm actually getting upset or if I'm still teasing. I just love this guy so much, and I couldn't love him like I do if I actually believe he'd do something like this to me.

"Yes, Ma'am!" he grins as he continues to drive, his eyes straight ahead, "I love you too, by the way."

Did I tell him I loved him? I mean, I do. At least, I think I do. When did I say it? Damn you, pain medicine. I wanted the first time we say it to be so special. Then it sinks in. He said it too! He loves me too! I look over to him, and he's grinning from ear to ear, but eyes fixed forward.

I'm floating on Cloud Nine, but it's clear neither of us is sure what to say next. Thankfully, we pull into my driveway, and that windshield won't save him from looking me in the eyes when we get to say it again.

##

"Oh, look what the cat dragged in. My food bowl is empty," Noah says as we walk in the front door, "Oh, I also threw up in the kitchen," he adds as he stops and turns to look back at me again, "What happened to you? You look like you lost at least one life!"

"Gee, thanks. I've been in the hospital for a week, and this is how you show me love when I get home. You kinda suck as a familiar. I liked you better when you didn't talk," I squat down to pet him so he knows I'm glad to see him too, "I can't believe you sometimes."

Josh puts his hand on my shoulder, "Hey, it's okay. I'll feed him and clean up the mess. You just sit down and relax."

"Thanks. I'm so happy I have you." I sit down on my couch and turn on the TV and start to search the menu for something romantic to watch. I realize that I've fallen asleep when Josh wakes me for dinner and to take my medicine.

"Thank you. I didn't realize how tired I was."

"It's okay. After you eat, you can go to bed. I'm thinking of inviting my family and your family over for a meet and greet. You know, to let them all get to know each other and get used to seeing us together. What do you think?

"I'd like that. In fact, I'd love it."

##

The next morning, I wake up and walk downstairs to see Josh making us breakfast. "Yes, Gram-Gram, her family is on their way, and you should be too. No, there shouldn't be any more Kathy drama. No, no, please don't bring any spell books. Because we don't need them. Okay, see you when you get here. Love you, Gram."

I walk up behind him and hug him, "So, was that Gram-Gram?" I can feel him shake with laughter.

"Yeah, she thinks she needs to bring all her spell books, and I told her she doesn't need to."

I realize I haven't called my parents, "I need to give them a call."

I watch Josh put eggs on a plate, "Don't worry, I already did it when you were asleep." I can't help but feel giddy inside as I realize just how much he's helped me the past week. While we are eating, I hear my doorbell ring.

"I got it," Josh says, getting up to walk to the door. When Josh opens the door,

I can hear my mother screaming with excitement, "Oh, well, look at you. So handsome! I like you already."

I get up, and before I get to the door, I can see my mother has Josh in a big hug. I laugh, "Hi, mom." I walk over, and she lets go of Josh and hugs me, "I've missed you. Where's Dad?" I ask while looking at the door.

"He had to work." I roll my eyes and drop a dramatic sigh, "The one time I want you guys to visit, he has to work? Well, come on, I see that you already met Josh. His Gram-Gram is coming soon," I smile and shut the front door.

"How have you been after everything with that witch? Are you eating, okay? Drinking enough water?"

"Yes, Mom, Josh has been a huge help with everything," I say as I wrap my arm around him and pull him in toward me.

Josh kisses my forehead and walks to my mother, "Want anything to eat or drink, ma'am?"

"That'll be *Mom* to you unless you two are a temporary thing," she says with a smile.

I look at Josh, who quickly affirms, "Mom, do you want anything to eat or drink?"

My mom gave a nod of approval, "I would love a glass of ice water, please."

"Yes, Mom, coming right up!"

I can see the worried expression on mom's face. "Well, I guess it's time to fill everyone in," I announce, and we all walk toward the living room.

"Here, mom, please sit." We start with the small stuff and then talk about Kathy and the whole dramatic mess.

"I'm so happy that you're okay. When Jewelz called me saying my baby was in the hospital, my imagination got the best of me. So, when Josh called me on your phone, I was so afraid he was going to tell me you'd passed on. Needless to say, when he said you were home and safe... Well, I'm just very relieved."

Josh excuses himself to refill Mom's water. I can't keep my eyes off him. He's always been super fun and nice, but seeing him in this setting just feels so right and natural. My heart swells with love, and all he's doing is refilling a glass of water.

"You love him, don't you?"

"Yeah, Mom, I do. I really do." I feel my eyes welling up, "It feels like my heart and soul are full when he's near me, and I'm scared to lose that feeling, mom. But with him, I can tell I won't. He makes me have butterflies in my stomach, and I feel safe when I'm in his arms. He makes me feel like a lovesick puppy."

I realize that I've been rambling as I focus back on my mom and see her smiling with tears in her eyes, "What's wrong, mom?" I ask, grabbing her hands.

"Nothing, dear. It's just that you're all grown up, and I don't quite know how to deal with it."

I smile and nod as Josh comes back in with a full glass of water, "Here you go, Mom." He looks at us, both with tears in our eyes, "Are you two okay?"

Mom smiles, "Yes, I'm just so happy that my daughter is finally happy and found someone that cares about her. She's lucky to have someone like you."

Josh hugs my mom, "No, I think I'm the lucky one. I was going to wait until later tonight, but I don't think I can." His expression changed from happy to something else.

I feel his energy, and there's anxiety and something heavy coming from him. Oh no, what's going on? Please tell me he's not going to break up.

Josh gets down on one knee and takes my hand, "Elizabeth, we've known each other for eight months, but to me, it feels like forever; and to me, forever sounds like a really good thing.

I want to be there when you are feeling low. I want to help you even when you don't need it. I want you in my life forever and always. I want to be wherever you are.

I want to be the one you run to when you don't know where else to go. But the most important thing is that I want to be your best friend forever. When I look into your eyes, I can see my home.

I see three of our kids running in the backyard with your eyes and smile, and I want to come home to you every day.

So, will you please make the happiest man alive and say yes?" He pulls out a ring with a rose-shaped diamond and holds his hand out to me.

"Yes, yes, I'll marry you!" I throw my arms around his neck and kiss him.

When we peel ourselves apart, I look at my mom, who's in tears, "Oh, mom," I grab her and give her a big hug, "So many tears today," she shakes her head, "Why do people cry when they're happy? We should be celebrating! "I'm so happy you found someone who loves you as much as I do."

##

We all stop talking when we hear Josh's phone going off. "Hello?" He looks up at me. His face turns ghostly pale, and he pushes the call to the speaker so I can hear as well.

"Sweetheart, this is Zeta, your Gram's neighbor. I don't know how to tell you this, but your grandmother was in the front yard about an hour ago, and someone in a white van came up and grabbed her. I tried to stop them, but it happened so fast I didn't know what to do."

I hear crying on the other end of the line. and I see Josh's face turn red, "I'll be over there as soon as possible. You did the right thing. I'll be right there."

He ends the call and looks at me, "I have to go back to Briarwood Flats. My grandmother has been abducted."

## About the Author

Brookelan Ables is from Sallisaw, Oklahoma. She's always been into supernatural and witchy stories, as well as the occasional romance.

Her love of reading stories about a girl and a guy meeting and falling in love created a passion for storytelling and coming up with fun and entertaining twists.

Brook says, "If someone had told me when I was younger, I would one-day author supernatural fiction, I would have laughed in their face. Now, seeing my dream come true, it's all so amazingly surreal.

Thanks to the *I'm the Writer* program, I am living my dream!

**Stay in the loop and get some fun nuggets by following Brooke at:**
https://www.facebook.com/brookeablesauthor
Twitter @brookelanray70
Instagram Brookie_cookie99

## Also From TLM Publishing House

**FICTION:**

The Mall Cadet Series

https://www.amazon.com/gp/product/B0B66M
DK3T

All In or Nothing Series

https://www.amazon.com/dp/B0B7FW9W8M

The 7 Wishes Series

https://www.amazon.com/dp/B0B62XJY59

The Deception Series

https://www.amazon.com/dp/B0B5RNQMF1

The Forbidden Love Series (18+)

https://www.amazon.com/dp/B0B5SX24SX

**NONFICTION:**

How to Start It Series

https://www.amazon.com/dp/B09Y2QHDPM

# Ready to share your story with the world?

I'm the writer publishing professional certification program that will teach you how to craft a fiction story so you can become a ghostwriter or share your own stories with the world.

For more info, go to
https://www.writercertification.com